Journeys to Bethlehem

Journeys to Bethlehem

the story of the first Christmas

Retold by Dorothy Van Woerkom
Art by Dhimitri Zonia

Concordia Publishing House
St. Louis   London

FOR MY GODPARENTS

Concordia Publishing House, St. Louis, Missouri
Concordia Publishing House Ltd., London, E. C. 1
Copyright © 1974 Concordia Publishing House
ISBN 0-570-03432-9

Manufactured in the United States of America

Nathanael said to him, "Can anything good come out of Nazareth?" Philip said to him, "Come and see."

John 1:46 RSV

Moonlight flashed against the Roman soldier's helmet as he urged his horse up the narrow trail. Near the top of the hill, among the shadows of tall cypress, he could see the square white houses.

So this was Nazareth! The soldier was impatient and tired. Twice he had lost his way to this nuisance of a place. Well, no matter that it was late and the people were asleep—was he to wait in the hills until cock-crow? No! He would waken them.

"Arise!" he shouted above the clatter of his horse's hooves. above the cackle of startled chickens, above the bleat of frightened lambs. "Arise and listen, in the name of Caesar!"

In fear and amazement the people hurried to the market place. There, by torchlight, the soldier read the decree from Caesar Augustus that they should all be counted and taxed. "Each must go to his own city," the soldier said. "Each to the city of his fathers. Make haste, Nazarenes, to obey the command of the Emperor!"

He gave them neither smile nor nod but rolled up his scroll and spurred his horse to a gallop down the road.

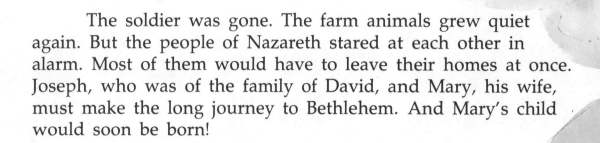

The soldier was gone. The farm animals grew quiet again. But the people of Nazareth stared at each other in alarm. Most of them would have to leave their homes at once. Joseph, who was of the family of David, and Mary, his wife, must make the long journey to Bethlehem. And Mary's child would soon be born!

Joseph walked slowly back to his house.

But Mary was already preparing for the journey. She had set out some round cheeses and small loaves of bread. From the wall she took down the goatskins which they would fill with water from the well in the morning. She saw how sad Joseph looked.

"Do not fear for me," she told him.

"Then try to sleep," he said. "It is a while yet to sunrise."

So Mary returned to her pallet, while Joseph stood at the open doorway, praying in the moonlight.

They left Nazareth at dawn, Mary riding on the donkey and Joseph leading it gently down the hillside. The trail twisted and turned through the mountains and olive groves of Galilee, until at last it joined the hilly caravan road high above the Jordan River.

There were many people on the road, all going to be counted. Some hurried quickly by, with sandals flapping and walking sticks sharply tapping the hard dirt. Some plodded wearily behind oxcarts loaded with all their possessions. Others drove their sheep and goats ahead of them, having no one left at home to care for them.

Towards evening of the fourth day, Joseph suddenly stopped and pointed. On a distant hill was Bethlehem.

It was late when they entered the busy, noisy town. Wagons and carts crowded the narrow street. Camels and donkeys pawed the ground. People knocked at shop doors to bargain with the merchants for a room, because the inn was full.

"The inn is full! No room, no room!" Joseph, pushing his way into the courtyard, dragging the donkey, heard the innkeeper shout it. Still he pushed on, shouldering his way through the crowd.

He pounded on the door. No answer. He pounded harder. His great, calloused, carpenter's hands shook the heavy door on its pivots. The upper half swung open.

"Well?" demanded the innkeeper. "Did I not just say there is no room? Have you left your ears behind you in the country?"

Then he hesitated. Joseph's eyes were burning into his. Mary, pale and tired on the weary little donkey, made him suddenly anxious to help. Gently he said, "Go around to the back. There you will find a cave. It is a stable, but you will not do better anywhere in Bethlehem tonight."

The air had turned cool after sunset. Now it was bitter cold. How much warmer the cave was than the courtyard! Mary smiled up at Joseph.

"We will be safe here," she said. "The Babe will be safe here."

Joseph was looking around the cave. "See the manger," he said. "It has a crooked leg, but I can fix that. It will make a comfortable bed for the Child."

Two sleepy oxen and a donkey drew nearer to watch while Joseph mended the manger and Mary smoothed out the hay for a bed.

At midnight, Jesus was born. Mary wrapped Him in a long linen cloth, and Joseph laid Him gently in the manger. Together they cared for Him and watched over Him through the night.

In the hills not far from Bethlehem, shepherds huddled around a small fire. Thousands of stars filled the clear night sky. Now and then a shepherd yawned or spoke softly to another. Here and there on the hillside a lamb called out to its mother. And over all came the sad sweet music of the flute played by a shepherd sitting apart from the others on a rock.

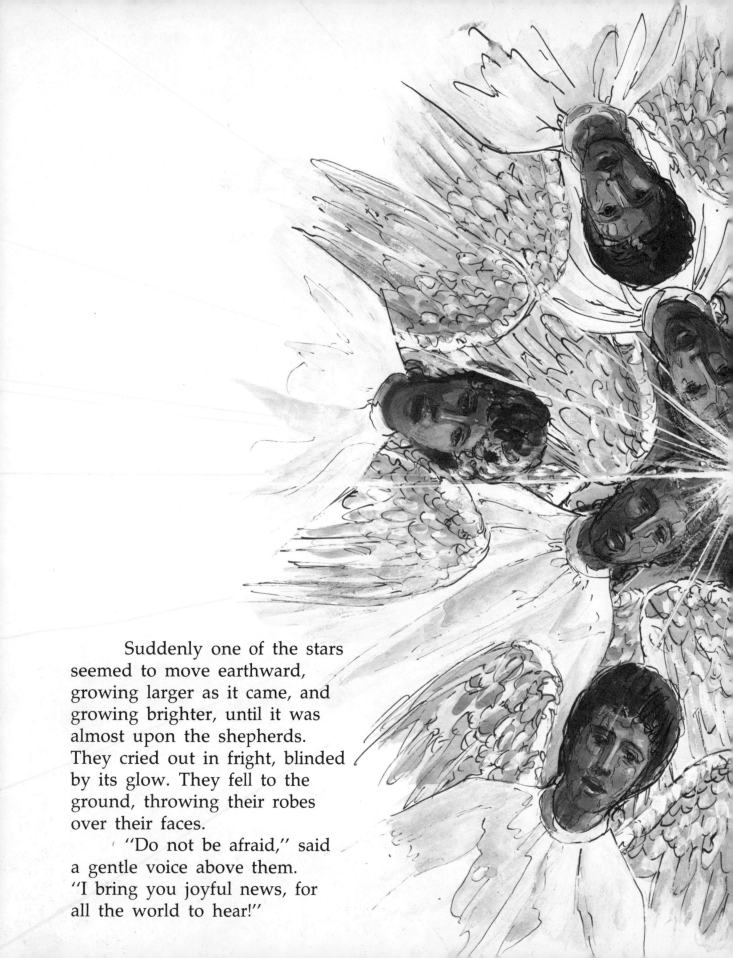

Suddenly one of the stars
seemed to move earthward,
growing larger as it came, and
growing brighter, until it was
almost upon the shepherds.
They cried out in fright, blinded
by its glow. They fell to the
ground, throwing their robes
over their faces.

"Do not be afraid," said
a gentle voice above them.
"I bring you joyful news, for
all the world to hear!"

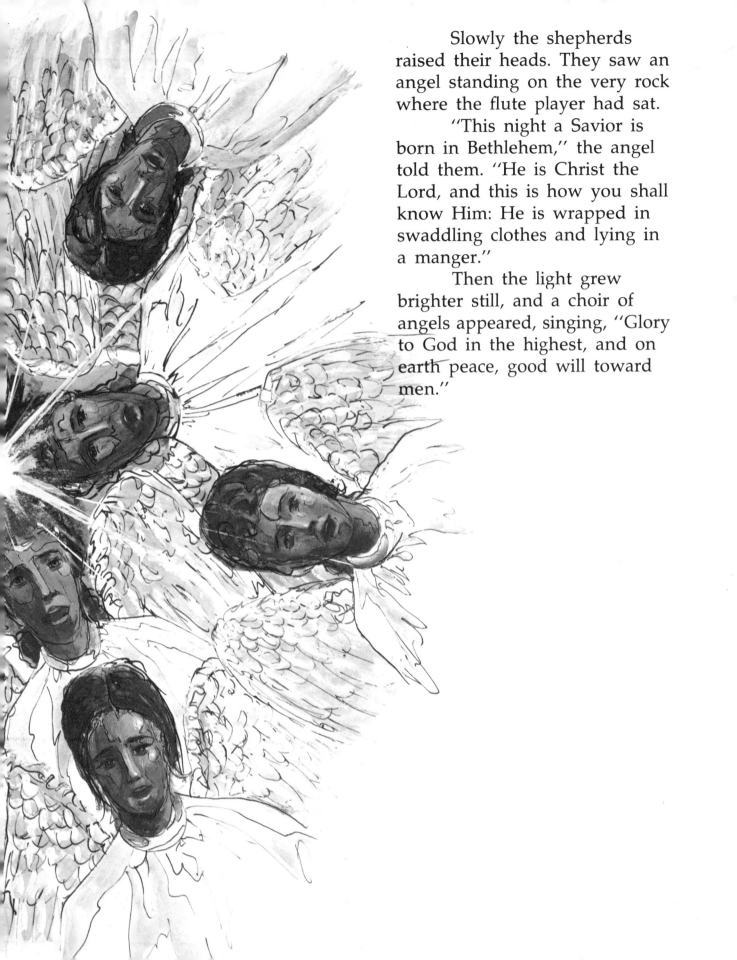

Slowly the shepherds raised their heads. They saw an angel standing on the very rock where the flute player had sat.

"This night a Savior is born in Bethlehem," the angel told them. "He is Christ the Lord, and this is how you shall know Him: He is wrapped in swaddling clothes and lying in a manger."

Then the light grew brighter still, and a choir of angels appeared, singing, "Glory to God in the highest, and on earth peace, good will toward men."

The angels disappeared with the last soft notes of their song, and the strange light faded. Once more the sky was clear and still. Yet the shepherds knelt in silence, until one of them cried,

"Let us go to Bethlehem and see this marvelous thing!"

So they drew lots for someone to stay behind with the sheep. The others hurried down to the town to find the Child in the manger. And, when they had found Him, they stopped all who would listen, to tell them the news of the Holy Child and what the angels had said of Him.

Now on the same midnight that Jesus was born, three Wise Men, who lived in a country far to the east, were watching the sky. They saw two strange stars moving toward each other. At last, on the eastern rim of the horizon, the stars came together. They formed a great ball of light, sweeping upwards across the sky, then moving slowly westward.

One of the Wise Men remembered that the Jews
believed a king would soon be born to them. Perhaps this
new star was the sign of his coming. They would go and see.

The way was long. They traveled by night, for they
could not see the star by day. Yet each evening at twilight
it appeared, leading them through hill and desert, through
rain and moonlight, through stillness and wind.

In Judea they stopped at Jerusalem, which they knew was the Holy City of the Jews. Certainly this was where their King would be born!

"Where is He that is born King of the Jews?" they asked again and again. "For we have seen His star in the East and have come to worship Him."

No one in Jerusalem had heard of such a King; but the cruel and wicked King Herod soon enough heard of the Wise Men! Herod stamped about his palace in a rage. Who was this, come to take his place? Who dared to call Himself King of the Jews?

Then Herod, also, remembered the Jewish prophecy about a king. He sent for his chief advisors.

"Tell me," he demanded, "where this King of Israel will be born."

They answered, "The Scriptures say in Bethlehem of Judea."

So Herod sent for the Wise Men and questioned them. They told him about the wonderful star and about the Child they sought.

"Then look in Bethlehem," Herod said, "and when you find Him, come and tell me, so that I may worship Him also."

But that night, while the Wise Men followed the star to Bethlehem, Herod plotted to kill the Child when they found Him.

The star did not lead to a palace as the Wise Men expected, but when they saw Jesus, they knew He was the King they had come to see. Bowing before Him, they offered their gifts of gold and frankincense and myrrh.

And when it came time to leave, an angel warned them in a dream that they should not return to Herod. They obeyed, going home by another way.

Then the angel came to Joseph. "Rise!" he said. "Herod's soldiers come to kill the Child. Flee from here at once! Take the Child and His mother to Egypt."

Joseph awoke at once. He saddled the donkey while Mary packed the saddlebags. They were on their way before daybreak. Hurrying across the hills and plains and desert, they traveled by night, rested by day, until at last they reached the safety of Egypt.

Time passed, and yet more time, until the angel came again, to tell Joseph of Herod's death.

King Herod was gone! Now they could return to Bethlehem! But when they came near Judea, they heard that Herod's son was king.

The son was as cruel as the father, and Joseph was afraid to remain in that country. He decided, instead, to follow the ancient road across the Plains of Sharon, northward into Galilee. He was bringing Mary and her Child to Nazareth—that little town so hidden in the hills that the Roman soldier nearly did not find it.

That what was spoken by the prophets might be fulfilled: "He shall be called a Nazarene."

Matthew 2:23 RSV